# A Note to Parents

DK READERS is a compelling program for beginning readers, designed in conjunction with leading literacy experts, including Dr. Linda Gambrell, Professor of Education at Clemson University. Dr. Gambrell has served as President of the National Reading Conference and the College Reading Association, and has recently been elected to serve as President of the International Reading Association.

Beautiful illustrations and superb full-color photographs combine with engaging, easy-to-read stories to offer a fresh approach to each subject in the series. Each DK READER is guaranteed to capture a child's interest while developing his or her reading skills, general knowledge, and love of reading.

The five levels of DK READERS are aimed at different reading abilities, enabling you to choose the books that are exactly right for your child:

**Pre-level 1:** Learning to read
**Level 1:** Beginning to read
**Level 2:** Beginning to read alone
**Level 3:** Reading alone
**Level 4:** Proficient readers

The "normal" age at which a child begins to read can be anywhere from three to eight years old. Adult participation through the lower levels is very helpful for providing encouragement, discussing storylines, and sounding out unfamiliar words.

No matter which level you select, you can be sure that you are helping your child learn to read, then read to learn!

LONDON, NEW YORK, MUNICH,
MELBOURNE, AND DELHI

**Editor** Hannah Dolan
**Designer** Rhys Thomas
**Senior Designer** Rob Perry
**Managing Art Editor** Ron Stobbart
**Art Director** Lisa Lanzarini
**Publishing Manager** Catherine Saunders
**Associate Publisher** Simon Beecroft
**Category Publisher** Alex Allan
**Production Editor** Clare McLean
**Production Controller** Nick Seston

**Reading Consultant**
Linda B. Gambrell, Ph.D.

First published in the United States in 2011
by DK Publishing
375 Hudson Street, New York, New York 10014

11 12 13 14 15  10 9 8 7 6 5 4 3
005

DK books are available at special discounts when purchased in bulk
for sales promotions, premiums, fund-raising, or educational use.
For details, contact:
DK Publishing Special Markets
375 Hudson Street
New York, New York 10014
SpecialSales@dk.com

A catalog record for this book is available
from the Library of Congress.

ISBN: 978-0-7566-7704-6 (Paperback)
ISBN: 978-0-7566-7705-3 (Hardcover)

Color reproduction by MDP
Printed and bound in the U.S.A. by Lake Book Manufacturing, Inc.

Discover more at
# www.dk.com

# www.LEGO.com

# DK READERS

BEGINNING TO READ ALONE

2

LEGO Kingdoms

# DEFEND THE CASTLE

Written by Hannah Dolan

Welcome to the Lion Kingdom!
It is in a land full of beautiful
lakes and mountains.

This is the Lion King.
He is the ruler of the
Lion Kingdom.

The Lion King is a good king.
The Lion Kingdom is a happy
place to live.

This is the Lion King's castle.

The Dragon Kingdom is in a land
just over the mountains.
It is not such a nice place to live.

This evil wizard
rules the Dragon
Kingdom.

The Dragon Wizard likes the Lion
Kingdom and he wants it for himself!

## Magic men
Wizards make magic
spells and potions.
They can use them
for good or evil.

The Dragon Wizard has a huge
Dragon Knight army.
These fierce soldiers are part of it.
The Dragon Knight army wants to
do battle to win the Lion Kingdom!

evil dragon
symbol

All the soldiers wear black and green.
That is to show they are part of the
Dragon Knight army.
The Dragon Knight army's special
symbol is an evil dragon.

The Lion King is not scared of the
Dragon Knight soldiers!
He has a mighty army of his own.
The King's army protects the
Lion Kingdom from enemies.
It keeps the King and his castle safe.

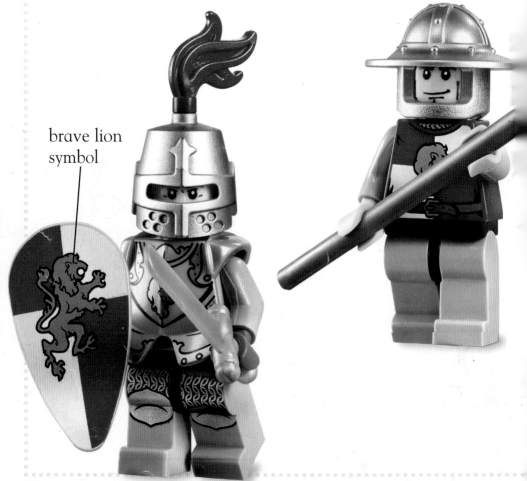

brave lion
symbol

All the King's soldiers wear red
and white.
The King's army's special symbol
is a brave lion.

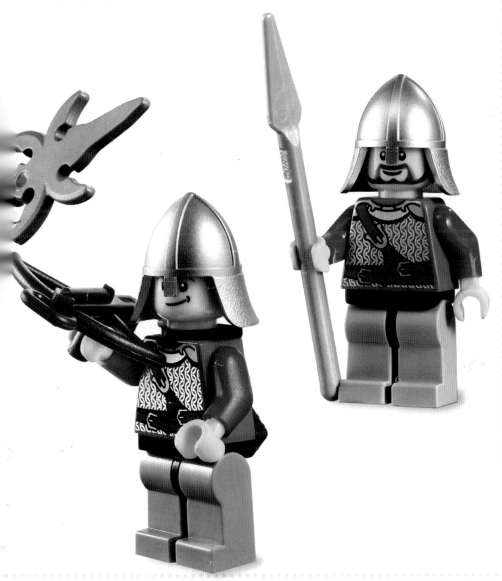

Battles can be
very dangerous
and soldiers
can get hurt.
Soldiers wear
tough armor so
that doesn't
happen.

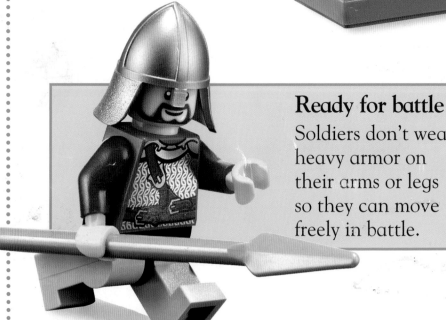

**Ready for battle**
Soldiers don't wear
heavy armor on
their arms or legs
so they can move
freely in battle.

Armor protects soldiers from
weapons like these spears.

spear

Armor is made from metal.
It is very heavy so soldiers must
be strong just to wear it.
Doing battle in it is even harder!

The Lion King's castle also needs
to be protected in battle.
It has tall towers called turrets.
The King's soldiers watch out for
enemies from the turrets.

Can you see the
giant catapult?
It is always ready
for action.
Whoosh!

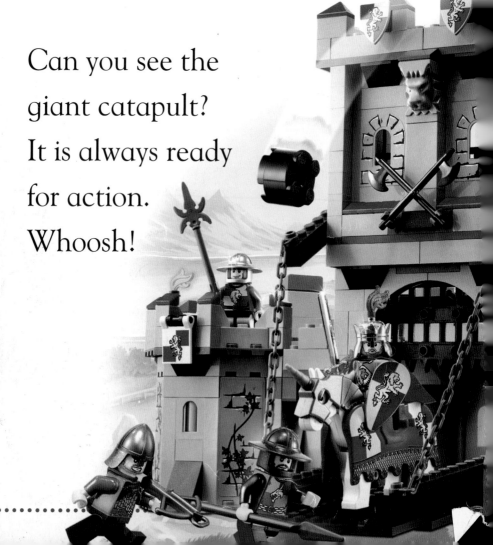

## The King's catapults

A catapult is a
fearsome weapon.
It can throw huge rocks
a very long way!

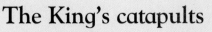

catapult

Let's go inside the Lion King's castle!
You will have to cross the castle's
drawbridge first.

**Quick draw**

A drawbridge is a special bridge with chains attached so it can be moved up or down.

Can you see the water around the castle? That is called a moat.
If the King's soldiers pull up the drawbridge, their enemies won't be able to get into the castle.
They will splash into the moat!

This is the King's jester.
His job at the castle is to entertain
the Lion King.

ometimes being the King is a tough job. He never knows when the Dragon Knight army will attack next.

The jester juggles balls and tells silly jokes to make the King and his soldiers laugh.

This man works at the castle, too.
He is a swordmaker.

He shapes metal into swords for
the King's soldiers to use in battle.

### Hot metal

The swordmaker heats up hard metal to make it soft so it is easier to shape into a sword.

Many of the King's soldiers use swords in battle. Others use spears and axes.

ax

outpost

At the entrance to the Lion Kingdom there is a big tower called an outpost.

It is the first thing enemies see if they come to the Lion Kingdom. The King's soldiers must guard the outpost to make sure no enemies can get past it.

## On guard
Soldiers take turns to be on guard duty so the outpost is always protected.

The Dragon Knight soldiers
are attacking the outpost with
their big catapult!
Can the King's soldiers defend it?

Oh no! These Dragon Knight soldiers have gotten past the King's outpost. They want to capture the King's soldiers and throw them in their special prison carriage!

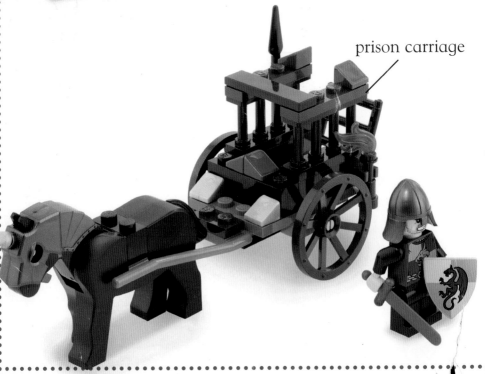

prison carriage

The prison carriage has big metal bars on it so captured King's soldiers can't escape.

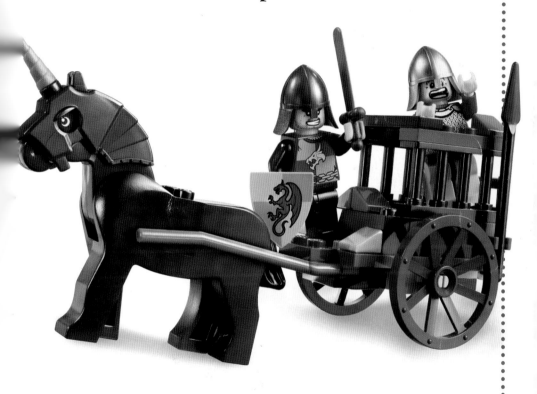

A powerful horse pulls the prison carriage along.

The Dragon Knight soldiers can speed away with their prisoner!

This is the King's knight.

He is the King's best soldier!

He wears special shining armor and rides a magnificent white horse.

He does important jobs for the King.

**A knight's tale**

A knight is a true hero.
No job is too dangerous
for him and he is very
brave in battle.

This King's soldier is very pleased
to see the King's knight!
The knight rescues him from the
Dragon Knights' prison carriage.

Be careful here! This is the evil Dragon Wizard's tower.

The King's knight has battled the Dragon Knight soldiers and sent them running back to the tower.

The tower has a heavy gate and a catapult but the brave King's knight isn't worried.

He warns the defeated Dragon Knight army to stay away from the Lion Kingdom in future.

Have you enjoyed your time in the world of LEGO® Kingdoms? Perhaps you could become a brave soldier or even a knight one day.

The Lion King says you are
welcome back to the Lion
Kingdom any time.
Maybe he will need your
help if the evil Dragon
Wizard attacks the
Lion Kingdom
again.

Goodbye,
good
King!

# Quiz!

1. Who is this?

2. What is a moat?

3. What does a jester do?

4. Why do you heat up metal to make a sword?